Five Homes for Five Kittens

written by Marie H. Frost
illustrated by Mikki Klug

Tracy's cat, Minerva, had kittens.

Tracy gave each kitten a name.
Tiger has stripes like a tiny tiger.
Smokey is gray like smoke.
Cocoa is brown like cocoa.
Mittens has four white paws.
Snowball is soft and white like snow.
Blackey is as black as night.

Can you count the kittens?
Can you point to each kitten and say its name?

Tracy thought each kitten was special.
She loved all the kittens.
But Mother and Daddy said,
"Too many kittens.
Too much noise!

You may keep only Minerva
and one kitten."

Tracy had a hard time choosing one kitten.
Which one do you think she chose?
Point to that kitten. What is its name?

"Now, what shall we do with the other kittens?" asked Mother.

"I will take them to my friends," said Tracy.

"How will you know which friends will make the best homes for the kittens?" asked Mother.

"God will help me decide," said Tracy.

What did Tracy do so God could help her decide?

Tracy talked to God.
She prayed, "Dear God, help me to take each kitten to the right home."

Down the street went Tracy with her little red wagon. Safely inside the basket were five little kittens.

Where do you suppose Tracy was going?

Mrs. White, who lived next door,
was planting flowers in her yard.
"Would you like a kitten for a pet?"
asked Tracy.

"Thank you," said Mrs. White.
"I do get lonely. A kitten would
be nice to cuddle in my lap."

Which kitten did Mrs. White choose?

Tracy pulled her wagon to the next house.
Mr. and Mrs. James were sitting
on their front porch, looking at
pictures of their grandchildren.

"Would you like a kitten?" asked Tracy.

"It's very kind of you to think of us,"
said Mrs. James.

"Our grandchildren would like to play
with a kitten when they come to visit,"
said Mr. James.

Which kitten did they choose?

Tracy turned the corner.
There was Mr. Douglas in the yard.
He was feeding his rabbits.
Tracy stopped to watch him.
Mr. Douglas had all kinds of animals—
a hamster,
two puppies,
five rabbits,
and a guinea pig.
"Would you like another pet—a kitten?"
asked Tracy.

"Always room for one more,"
said Mr. Douglas. "Thank you."

Which kitten did Mr. Douglas choose?

"I think I'll go to Missy's house," thought Tracy. "She always likes to play with Minerva. And today is Missy's birthday."

Tracy pulled her wagon to Missy's house. "Would you like a kitten?" asked Tracy.

"I'll ask Mother if I may have one," said Missy. And she ran into the house. When Missy came back, she looked happy. "Oh, yes, I'd like this one," said Missy.

Can you tell which kitten Missy chose?

Tracy had one kitten left.
"I know who needs this kitten,"
Tracy said. "Ryan Brown.
His kitten ran away last week."
Tracy hurried to Ryan's house.
Ryan was playing all by himself.
"Would you like a kitten?"
asked Tracy.

Ryan had a big smile on his face.
"Oh, thank you, Tracy.
Now I won't feel sad anymore."

What was the name of Ryan's kitten?

Tracy's kittens were all gone.
"Thank You, God," she whispered.
Mother was waiting for her at the door.
"Oh, Mother," said Tracy. "God helped
me find a special home for each kitten."
"I'm glad," said Mother.
And she hugged Tracy real hard!